FLEXI VIOLIN 1

Paul Harris and Jessica O'Leary

VIOLIN (SOLO AND ACCOMPANIMENT) PART

	Duet part	Solo part
First Solo Hans Sitt	2	3
March of the Women Ethel Smyth	2	3
Witches' Waltz Jessica O'Leary	4	5
Mazurka brillante Tekla Bądarzewska-Baranowska	4	5
Zickety, Dickety, Dock British traditional	6	7
Violin Concerto Op. 61 Ludwig van Beethoven	6	7
Bhangra Indian traditional	8	9
London Bridge is Falling Down British traditional	8	9
Rasa Sayang Indonesian traditional	10	11
Rondo Wolfgang Amadeus Mozart	10	11
Sophia Maria Theresia von Paradis	12	13
Isabel's Piece Paul Harris	12	13
Pastorella Fanny Mendelssohn	14	15
Rigadon Charles Dancla	16	17
Duetto Franz Schubert	18	19

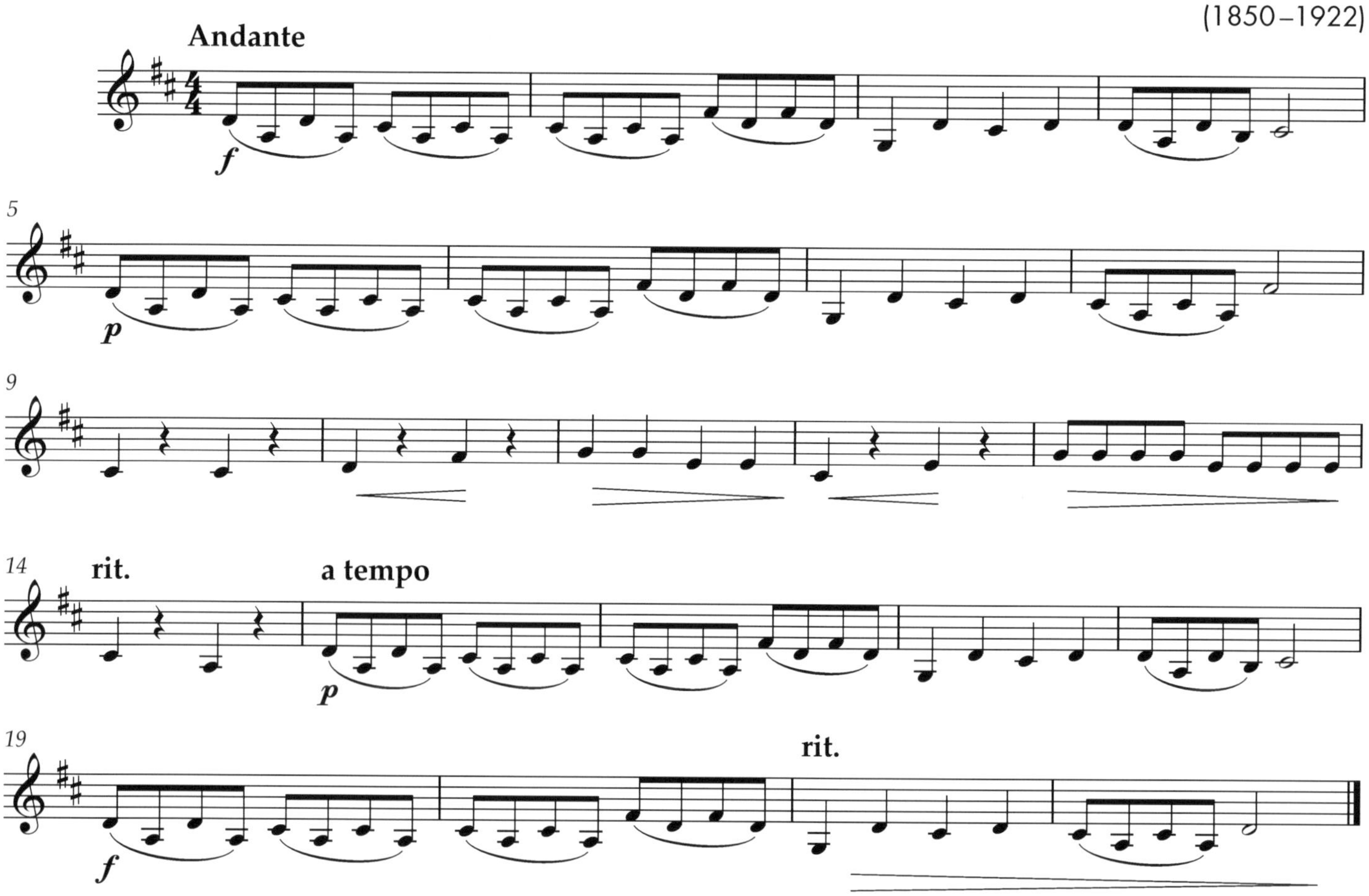

First Solo

Hans Sitt
(1850–1922)

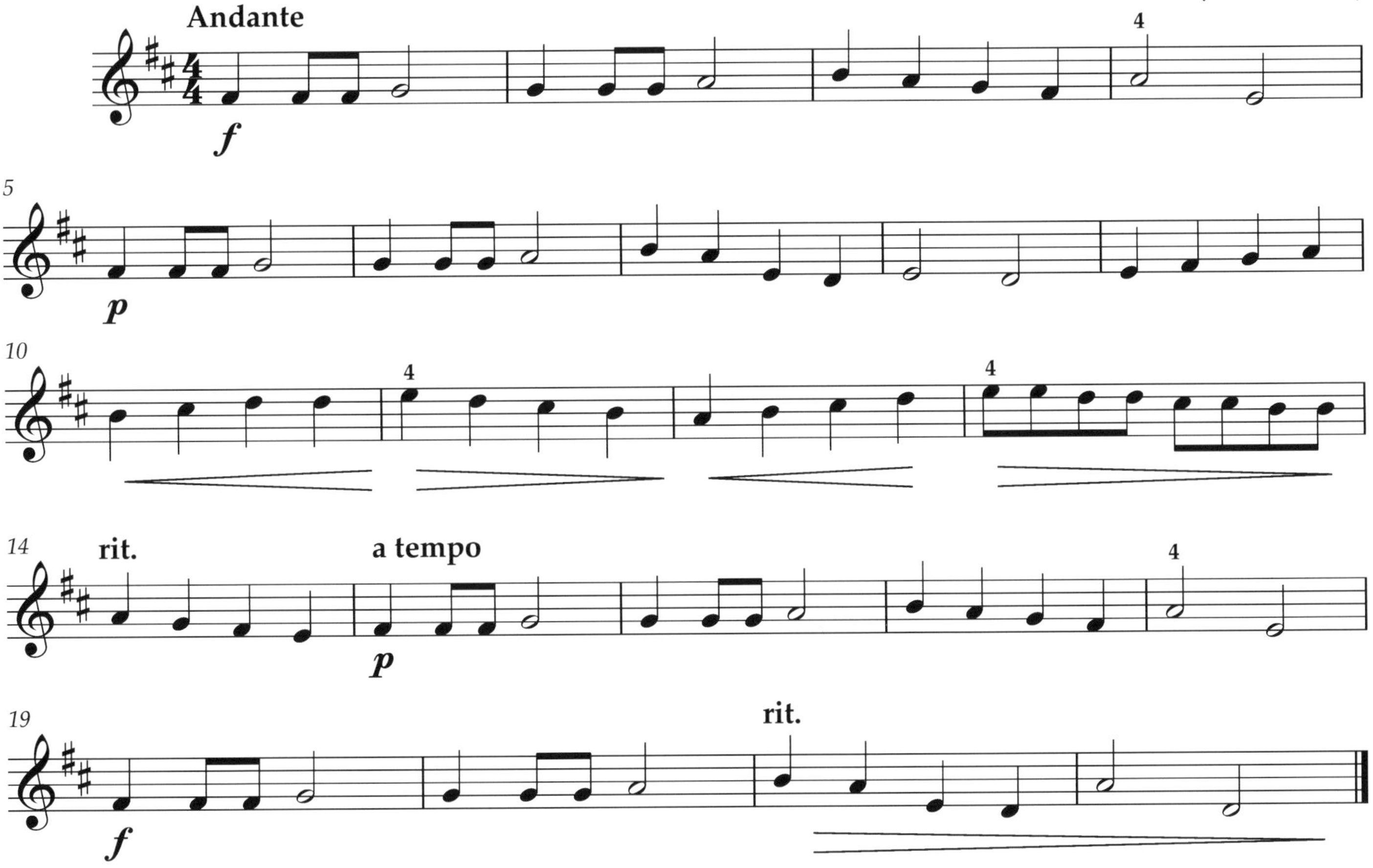

© 2022 by Faber Music Ltd.

March of the Women

Ethel Smyth
(1858–1944)

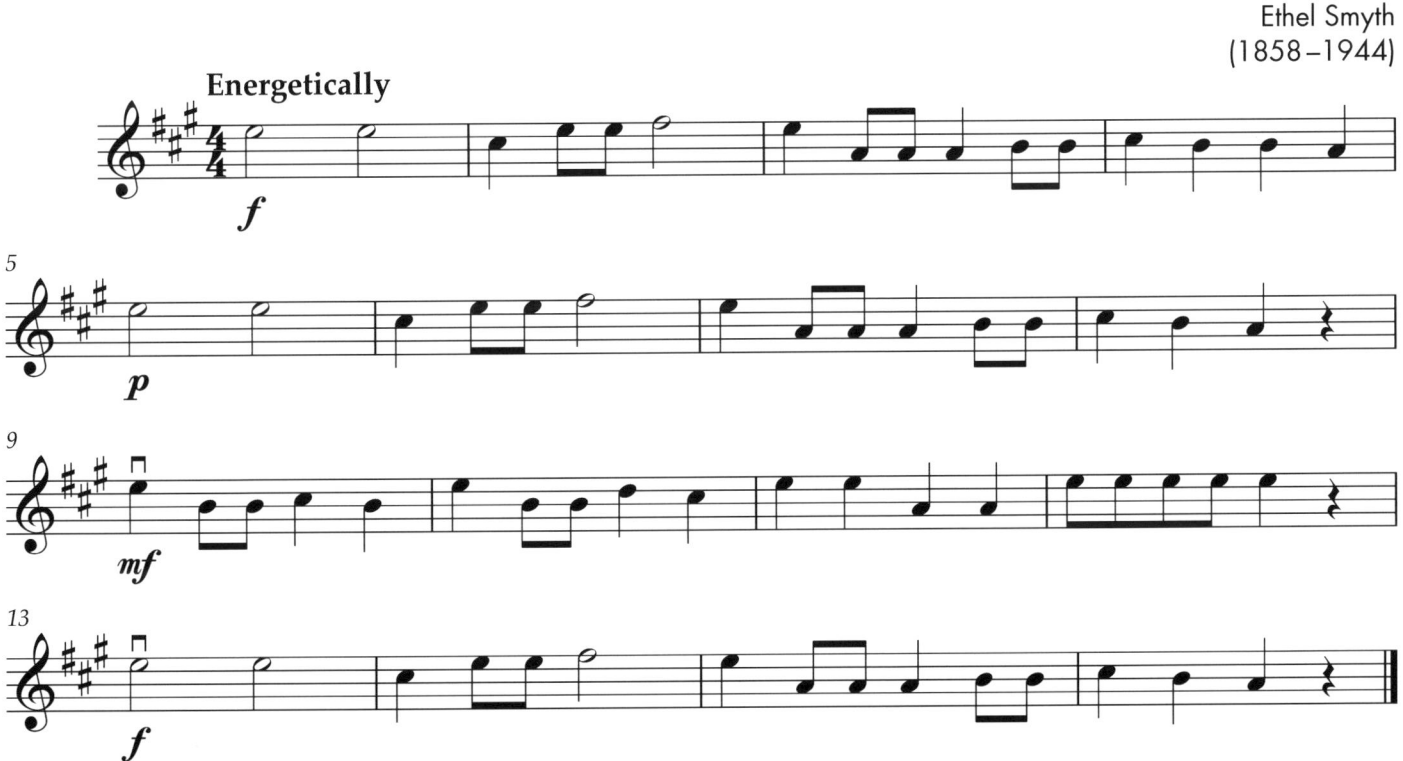

© 2022 by Faber Music Ltd.

Violin accompaniment

Witches' Waltz (duet part)

Jessica O'Leary

© 2022 by Faber Music Ltd.

Mazurka brillante (duet part)

Tekla Bądarzewska-Baranowska
(1834–1861)

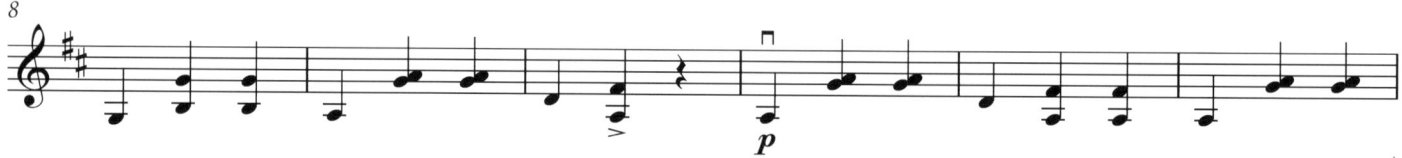

© 2022 by Faber Music Ltd.

Witches' Waltz

Jessica O'Leary

© 2022 by Faber Music Ltd.

Mazurka brillante

Tekla Bądarzewska-Baranowska
(1834–1861)

© 2022 by Faber Music Ltd.

Violin accompaniment

Zickety, Dickety, Dock (duet part)

British traditional

Violin Concerto Op. 61 (duet part)

Ludwig van Beethoven
(1770–1827)

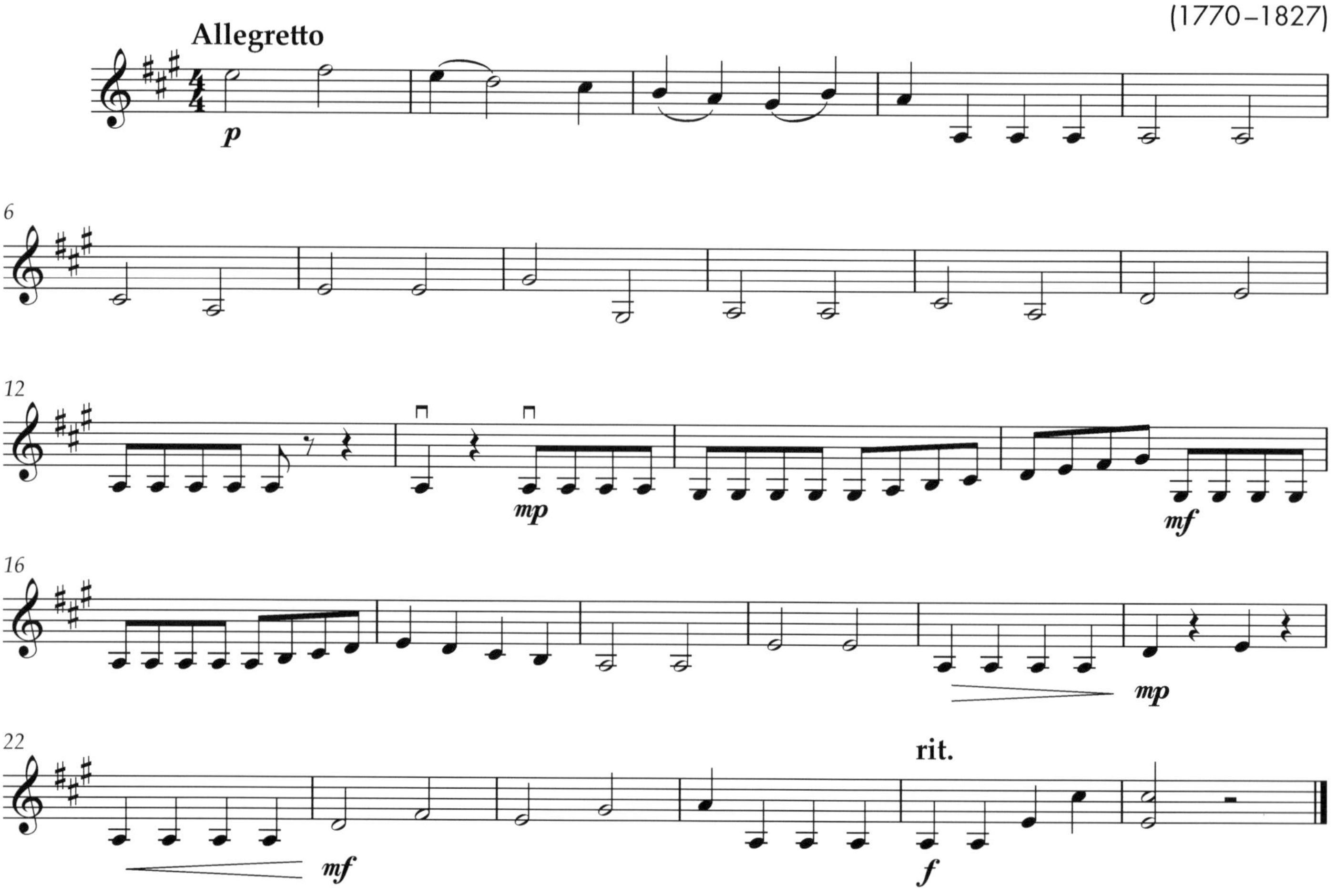

© 2022 by Faber Music Ltd.

Violin solo

Zickety, Dickety, Dock

British traditional

© 2022 by Faber Music Ltd.

Violin Concerto Op. 61

Ludwig van Beethoven
(1770–1827)

© 2022 by Faber Music Ltd.

Violin accompaniment

Bhangra (duet part)

Indian traditional

© 2022 by Faber Music Ltd.

London Bridge is Falling Down (duet part)

British traditional

© 2022 by Faber Music Ltd.

Bhangra

London Bridge is Falling Down

Violin accompaniment

Rasa Sayang (duet part)

Indonesian traditional

Rondo (duet part)

Wolfgang Amadeus Mozart
(1756–1791)

FLEXI VIOLIN 1

Paul Harris and Jessica O'Leary

PIANO ACCOMPANIMENT

FABER *ff* MUSIC

INTRODUCTION

The FLEXI VIOLIN series brings together a diverse range of enjoyable and colourful pieces for the developing violinist to study and perform. We've chosen the title Flexi because the pieces can be performed in a number of different ways: violin with piano accompaniment, violin duet (with the teacher or more advanced student playing the second part) or two violins and piano accompaniment. Every combination provides a complete and satisfying performance.

Jessica O'Leary and Paul Harris

© 2022 by Faber Music Ltd
This edition first published in 2022
Bloomsbury House, 74–77 Great Russell Street, London WC1B 3DA
Music processed by Jackie Leigh
Cover design by Chloë Alexander Design
Printed in England by Caligraving Ltd
All rights reserved

ISBN10: 0-571-54269-7
EAN13: 978-0-571-54269-7

To buy Faber Music publications or to find out about the full range of titles available please contact your local music retailer or Faber Music sales enquiries:

Faber Music Ltd, Burnt Mill, Elizabeth Way, Harlow CM20 2HX
Tel: +44 (0) 1279 82 89 82
fabermusic.com

CONTENTS

First Solo Hans Sitt   4

March of the Women Ethel Smyth   6

Witches' Waltz Jessica O'Leary   7

Mazurka brillante Tekla Bądarzewska-Baranowska   8

Zickety, Dickety, Dock British traditional   10

Violin Concerto Op. 61 Ludwig van Beethoven   12

Bhangra Indian traditional   14

London Bridge is Falling Down British traditional   16

Rasa Sayang Indonesian traditional   18

Rondo Wolfgang Amadeus Mozart   20

Sophia Maria Theresia von Paradis   22

Isabel's Piece Paul Harris   24

Pastorella Fanny Mendelssohn   26

Rigadon Charles Dancla   28

Duetto Franz Schubert   30

First Solo

Hans Sitt
(1850–1922)

March of the Women

Ethel Smyth
(1858–1944)

Witches' Waltz

Jessica O'Leary

© 2022 by Faber Music Ltd.

Mazurka brillante

Tekla Bądarzewska-Baranowska
(1834–1861)

Zickety, Dickety, Dock

British traditional

Violin Concerto Op. 61

Ludwig van Beethoven
(1770–1827)

13

Bhangra

Indian traditional

© 2022 by Faber Music Ltd.

London Bridge is Falling Down

British traditional

© 2022 by Faber Music Ltd.

Rasa Sayang

Indonesian traditional

Rondo

Wolfgang Amadeus Mozart
(1756–1791)

Sophia

Maria Theresia von Paradis
(1759–1824)

Isabel's Piece

Paul Harris

Pastorella

Fanny Mendelssohn
(1805–1847)

Rigadon

Charles Dancla
(1817–1907)

Duetto

Franz Schubert
(1797–1828)

* Play bracketed notes when no violin accompaniment.

© 2022 by Faber Music Ltd.

Violin solo

Rasa Sayang

Indonesian traditional

© 2022 by Faber Music Ltd.

Rondo

Wolfgang Amadeus Mozart
(1756–1791)

© 2022 by Faber Music Ltd.

Sophia (duet part)

Maria Theresia von Paradis
(1759–1824)

© 2022 by Faber Music Ltd.

Isabel's Piece (duet part)

Paul Harris

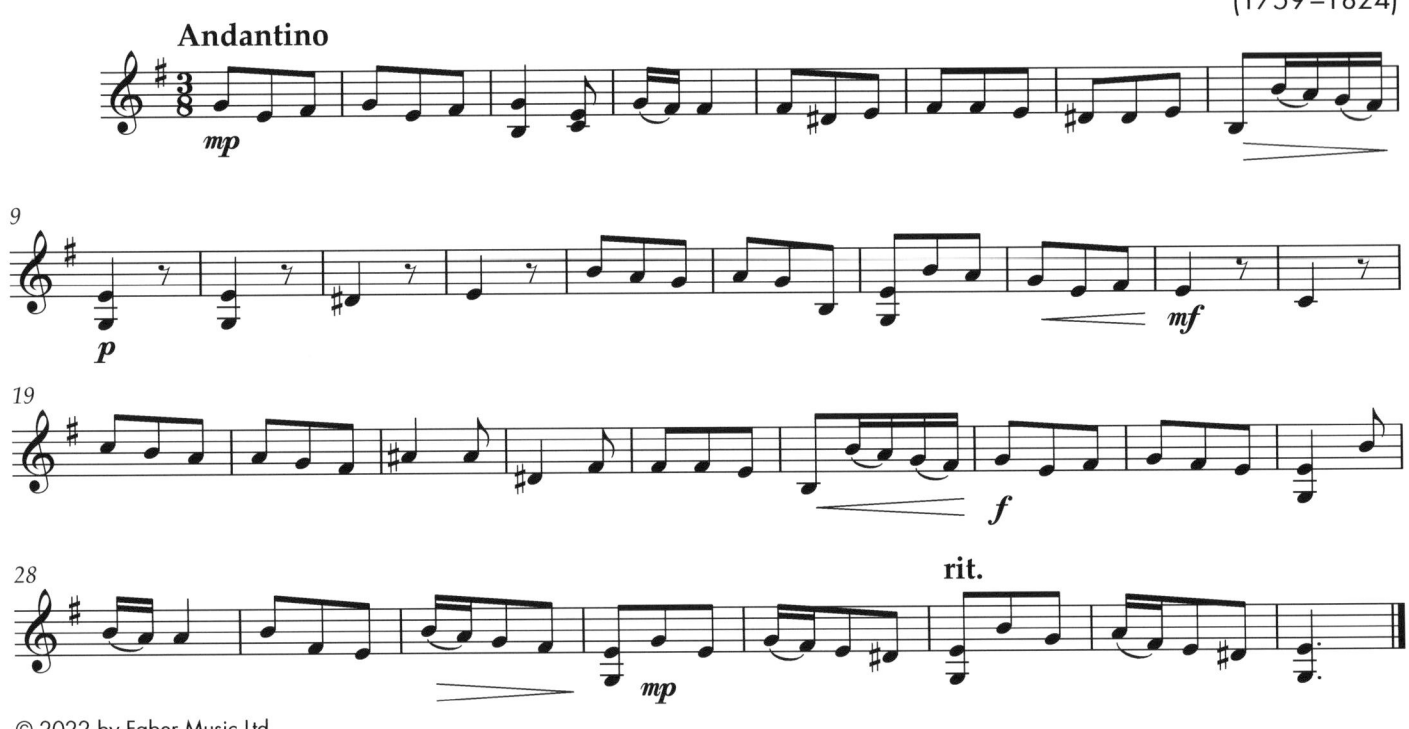

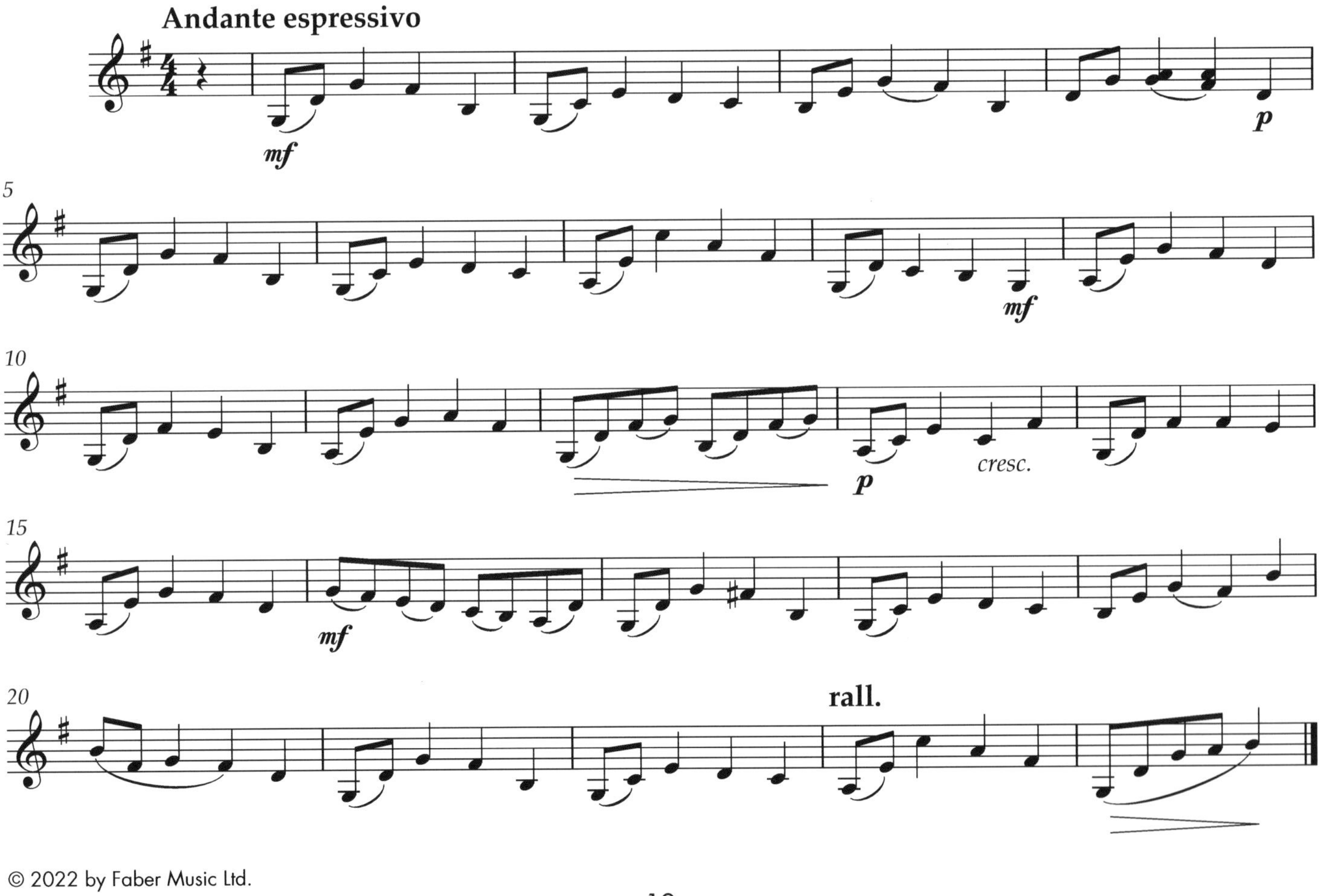

© 2022 by Faber Music Ltd.

Sophia

Maria Theresia von Paradis
(1759–1824)

© 2022 by Faber Music Ltd.

Isabel's Piece

Paul Harris

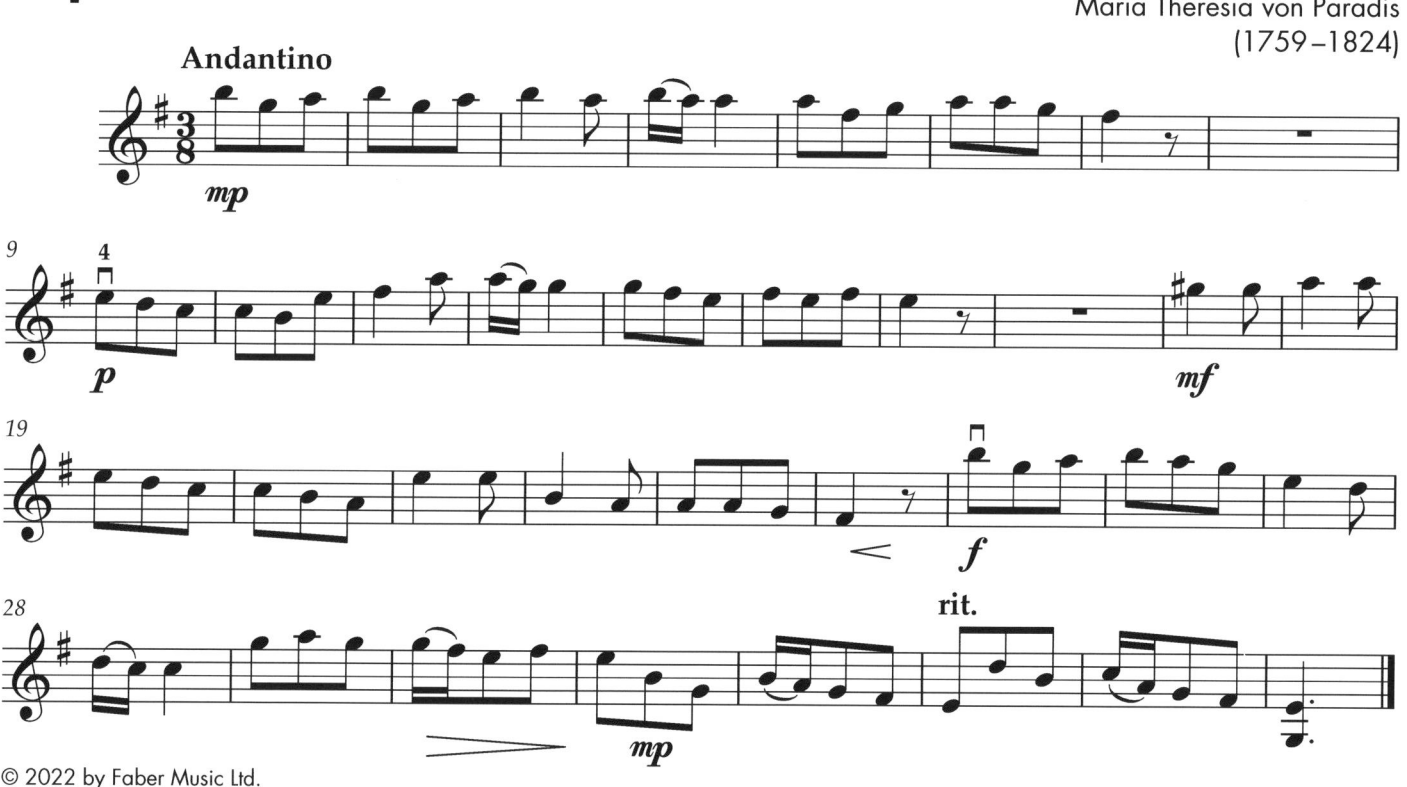

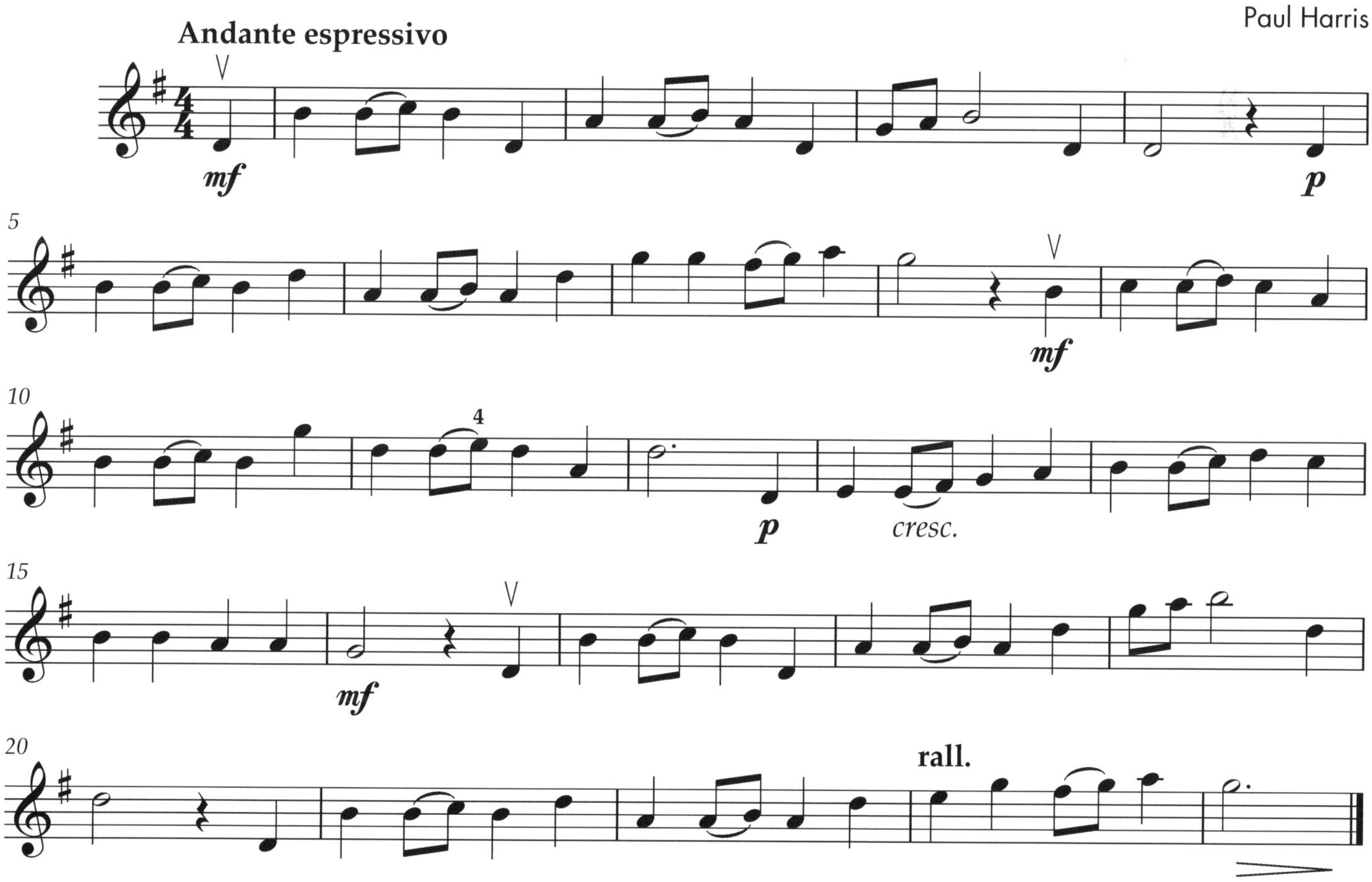

© 2022 by Faber Music Ltd.

Violin accompaniment

Pastorella (duet part)

Fanny Mendelssohn
(1805–1847)

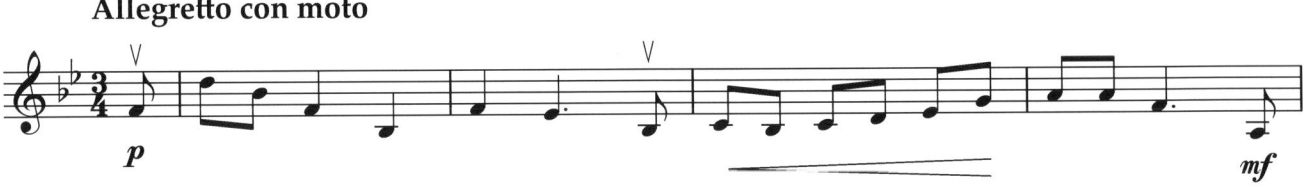

© 2022 by Faber Music Ltd.

Violin solo

Pastorella

Fanny Mendelssohn
(1805–1847)

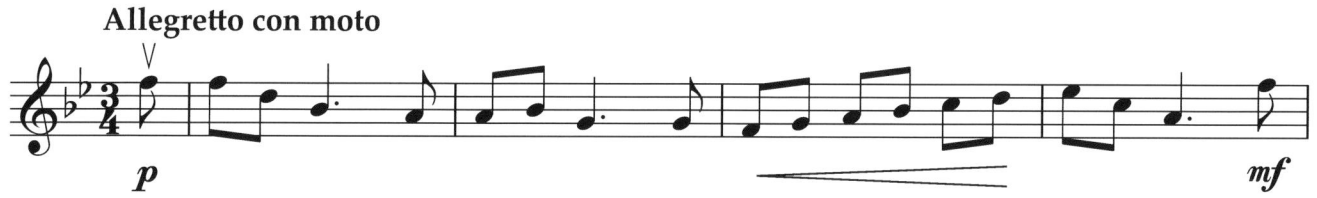

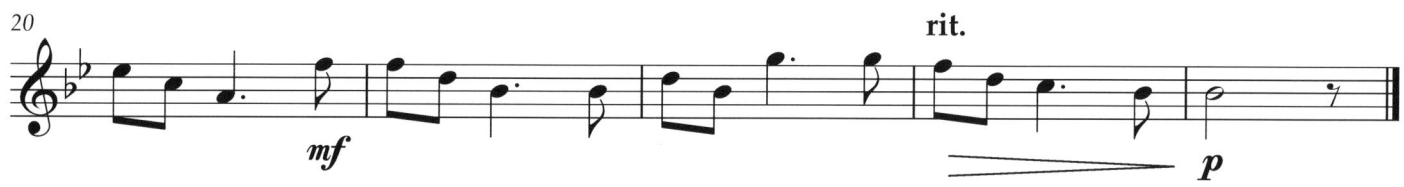

© 2022 by Faber Music Ltd.

Violin accompaniment

Rigadon (duet part)

Charles Dancla
(1817–1907)

© 2022 by Faber Music Ltd.

Violin solo

Rigadon

Charles Dancla
(1817–1907)

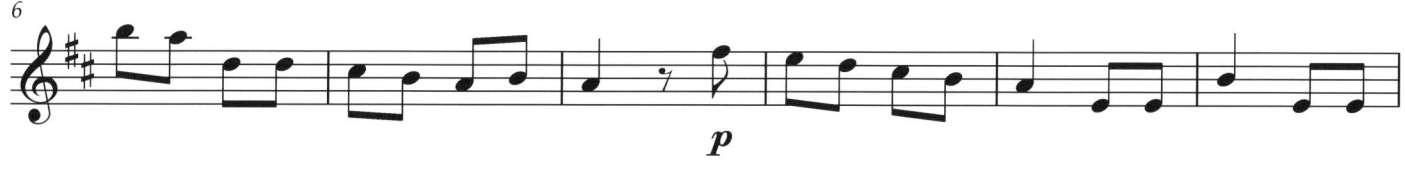

Violin accompaniment

Duetto (duet part)

Franz Schubert
(1797–1828)

INTRODUCTION

The FLEXI VIOLIN series brings together a diverse range of enjoyable and colourful pieces for the developing violinist to study and perform. We've chosen the title Flexi because the pieces can be performed in a number of different ways: violin with piano accompaniment, violin duet (with the teacher or more advanced student playing the second part) or two violins and piano accompaniment. Every combination provides a complete and satisfying performance.

Jessica O'Leary and Paul Harris

© 2022 by Faber Music Ltd
This edition first published in 2022
Bloomsbury House, 74–77 Great Russell Street, London WC1B 3DA
Music processed by Jackie Leigh
Cover design by Chloë Alexander Design
Printed in England by Caligraving Ltd
All rights reserved

ISBN10: 0-571-54269-7
EAN13: 978-0-571-54269-7

To buy Faber Music publications or to find out about the full range of titles available please contact your local music retailer or Faber Music sales enquiries:

Faber Music Ltd, Burnt Mill, Elizabeth Way, Harlow CM20 2HX
Tel: +44 (0) 1279 82 89 82
fabermusic.com